# THE PRINCE OF EGYPT

DREAMWORKS

ISBN: 0-525-46054-3 First Edition 2 4 6 8 10 9 7 5 3 1
Produced exclusively for Wal-Mart Stores, Inc.

Long ago, a mighty Pharaoh ruled the land of Egypt. He was a man of power and dreams, a man who saw himself through history's eyes. And so he sought to build an empire greater than any seen before. There would be giant monuments and temples in his honor, as if he himself were a god.

But large monuments are made of many bricks—and hard labor. Pharaoh Seti needed slaves to do his work. The slaves he found were Hebrews, for he saw that Egypt was filled with them. He set taskmasters over them, with whips to sting their shoulders as they lifted straw, sand, water, and mud to build glory to his name.

But when the Hebrew numbers grew, Seti became afraid of their strength. And so he devised a terrible solution. He sent his soldiers into Goshen, where the slaves lived, and ordered them to kill all the newborn Hebrew boys.

One Hebrew mother was brave enough to hide her infant boy for three months. But one day, the soldiers came too close. Together with her two older children, Miriam and Aaron, Yocheved made the hardest decision of all: to save her child, she must send him away.

*Hush now, my baby. Be still, love, don't cry.*

*Sleep as you're rocked by the stream.*

*Sleep and remember my last lullaby…*

*So I'll be with you when you dream.*

With that sweet song of prayer, the boy's mother laid him in a basket and set him adrift on the River Nile. Gently the water swept the basket and its precious cargo from her hands into the swift current.

But little Miriam would not let her baby brother out of sight. She ran along the river-bank, anxiously watching the basket's perilous journey. She gasped aloud when it swirled on a wave, dashing between a pair of battling hippos.

Yet whether by fate or by chance, the basket floated safely past this danger and many more. Snapping crocodiles, fishermen's nets, the bows of giant ships—none of these prevented the basket from staying on its protected course.

Indeed, the sweeping oars of a huge barge at last pushed the basket out of harm's way and sent it floating with sudden gentleness toward the very steps of Pharaoh's palace.

There in the water garden, the Queen, her handmaidens, and little Prince Rameses were taking their daily refreshment when the basket came to rest. Miriam gasped with fear as she watched the Queen herself draw the basket near and lift its lid.

With a soft cry of delight, the Queen gazed at the sweet cheeks and sleepy eyes of the baby nestled inside. "Come, Rameses," she said without hesitation. "We will show Pharaoh your new baby brother, Moses." And so the child had a new home, a new family, a new name.

Miriam was relieved and grateful to see the miracle of her brother's rescue. From her hiding place in the tall reeds, she echoed their mother's lullaby with her own song of hope. *"Grow, baby brother. Come back someday. Come and deliver us, too."*

The Pharaoh and the Queen treated Moses well, for they considered him a gift from the gods. They raised him alongside their own son, Rameses.

And in the eyes of his loving parents, Moses was equal to his brother in nearly all things: a true prince of Egypt. He lived in splendid rooms made of alabaster stone and perfumed with incense. Remembering no other, he was proud of his home. In it, he felt noble and strong.

Moses and Rameses grew up as boys do: studious in some things, reckless in others. One of their greatest pleasures was playing tricks on the palace priests, Hotep and Huy. Another was chariot racing.

"Hey, Rameses, how'd you like your face carved on a wall?

"Someday, yes."

"How about now?" Moses pulled his chariot sharply to the side, almost pinning Rameses against a temple wall.

"If it's fun you want..." Rameses said as he moved to retaliate. But Moses skidded to a stop, leaving Rameses' chariot to plummet down a sand dune. Laughing, the two boys were soon at it again, racing along another wall.

But the wall was not built to withstand the onslaught of two boys in chariots. It burst apart with a mighty force. A tidal wave of sand spilled down onto the plaza below, where Hotep and Huy were busy performing a ritual to sanctify the temple.

Moses and Rameses surfed down the mountain of cascading sand—which completely destroyed the temple and buried Hotep and Huy into the bargain.

"Why do the gods torment me with such reckless, destructive, blasphemous sons?" Seti was furious. Rameses started to answer, but Seti would not allow interruption. "I seek to build an empire, and your only thought is to amuse yourselves by tearing it down."

"The fault is mine," said Moses. "I goaded Rameses on, and so I am responsible."

"Responsible?" retorted Seti. "Do you know the meaning of that word, Rameses? When I pass into the next world, you will be the morning and evening star."

"One damaged temple does not destroy centuries of tradition," said Rameses defiantly.

"But one weak link can break the chain of a mighty dynasty," bellowed Seti. And with a wave of his arm, Seti dismissed his older son.

But Moses stayed and spoke to his father. "All he cares about is your approval. I know he will live up to your expectations. He only needs the opportunity."

Seti considered Moses' words and then dismissed him, too. "Go now," he said. "I shall see you both tonight."

"I can see it now," Moses said later, teasing his sulking brother. "There go the pyramids! Single-handedly you will manage to bring the greatest kingdom on earth to ruin." But Rameses refused to be cheered. Their father had hurt him deeply.

"Tell me this, Moses," he said, moving to the balcony where his brother stood. "Why is it that every time *you* start something, *I'm* the one who ends up in trouble?"

But Moses wasn't paying attention. Hotep and Huy were walking just below the balcony, and Moses had noticed a tempting bowl of pink fruit punch nearby. With a devilish look, he dropped a balloon filled with the liquid right onto their heads.

"Rameses, get down here! I think you owe us an apology!" yelled Huy.

"Oh, my new thing!" moaned Hotep. Moses handed Rameses the entire bowl of punch and said, "You might as well." Hotep and Huy were drenched again. The brothers enjoyed a good laugh—until Moses mentioned that they were probably late for their father's banquet.

Moses and Rameses tried
to sneak into the banquet hall.
But when the door opened,
they were greeted by a huge,
cheering throng.

"Ah, the young princes!" said the Queen, as if they were right on time. She hugged
Rameses and whispered, "You were just named Prince Regent. You are now responsible
for overseeing the temples." Then she turned to Moses and said, "Apparently, someone
thought he just needed the opportunity."

Moses stepped forward and shouted, "My Lord Pharaoh, I propose that the high
priests offer tribute to their new regent!" At that, the two magicians looked at each other
and grinned mischievously. "The Midian girl," said Hotep to Huy. "Go get her."

While Huy went backstage, Hotep began their magical presentation.

After a blast of smoke and the yank of a curtain, Hotep revealed a beautiful Midianite girl, bound at the wrists with a rope. "Let us inspect this desert flower," said Rameses.

But the girl was too strong for her captors. When Rameses approached her, she tried to bite him. "More like a desert cobra," said Rameses. Shrinking back, Rameses decided to give the girl to Moses instead, glad to be rid of her.

"I won't be given to anyone!" the girl exclaimed, pulling on the rope with all her strength. "Especially not to an arrogant, pampered palace brat! I demand you set me free." Moses watched as she backed toward a large reflecting pool. With a shrug, he let go of the rope, laughing as she fell into the water.

But later, when Moses saw that the Midianite girl had run away, he did not call the guards. Instead, he allowed her to escape from the palace and, intrigued, began to follow her.

Moses hurried down the darkened streets of Goshen, the small, cramped part of the city where the Hebrew slaves lived. He was far from the palace now. Moses had never had a reason to come to Goshen before.

Around a corner, he suddenly stopped, seeing the beautiful desert girl with a camel up ahead. From the shadows, he saw her approach two Hebrews, who were drawing water from a well.

"Please," the girl said. "I need water. I've a long journey ahead of me."

"May God protect you," the Hebrew woman replied.

As the girl led her camel off toward the desert, Moses came out of his hiding place and approached the well. His eyes were still following the Midianite girl, when the sound of a shattering pot brought his gaze abruptly to the Hebrew girl before him.

She gasped, "Oh! Oh, oh...I'm sorry.
I'm so sorry. I did not expect to see you...here...at last." It was Miriam, Moses' sister, now
grown up and overjoyed to see her younger brother. With her was Aaron, who feared to
watch this confrontation between his sister, a slave girl, and a prince of Egypt.

Joyfully, Miriam continued. "I knew you cared about our freedom."

"Freedom," Moses said, laughing. "Why would I care about that?"

"Because," said Miriam haltingly, "you're our brother..." She reached out to touch Moses' arm.
"Our mother set you adrift in a basket to save your life."

"Save my life? From whom?"

"Ask the man you call father," Miriam said bitterly.

"How dare you!" shouted Moses as he pushed her to the ground. With that, he turned
to walk away. But then something teased his memory—a voice both familiar and strange.
He stopped, stunned by all that stirred within him as he heard Miriam sing, *"Hush now, my
baby. Be still, love, don't cry"*—the same lullaby that his mother had sung long ago.

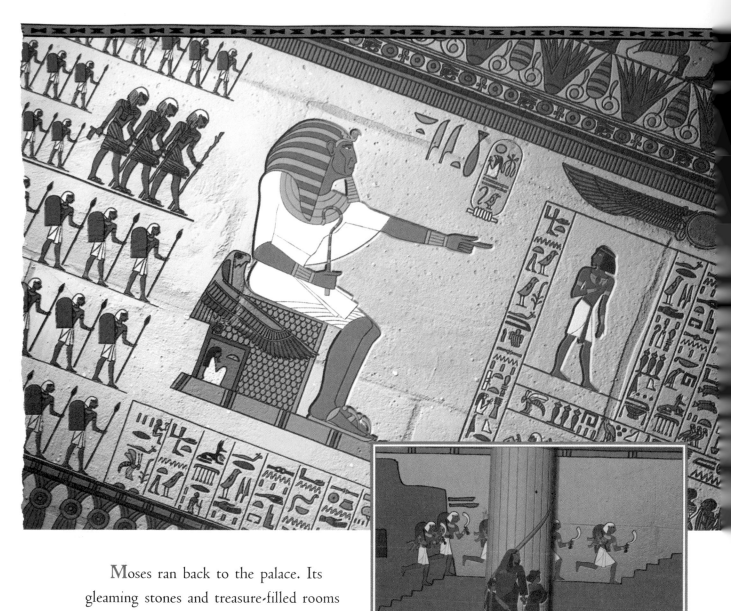

Moses ran back to the palace. Its gleaming stones and treasure-filled rooms should have reassured him. But the slave girl's words stuck in his thoughts—and then in his dreams.

Moses fell into a troubled sleep. He saw his father send soldiers with sickles into Goshen. He watched the soldiers as they snatched crying babies from the arms of Hebrew mothers.

And he saw Yocheved run down to the Nile with her little boy and set him adrift in a basket.

In his nightmare, he watched as the guards threw other babies into the Nile, where crocodiles waited with hungry jaws opened wide. Then Moses, too, tumbled down into the river, down toward those sharp teeth, a terrible sound ringing in his ears—until he awoke with a start.

Moses grabbed a torch and ran through the palace. For the first time, he truly saw the images that had always been there on the painted walls. Here were the crying babies. Here was his father, the mighty Pharaoh, ordering the guards to carry out his terrible decree. It was all as he had seen in his nightmare—and as the slave girl had said.

Moses fell to his knees. Then he felt the touch of a hand on his head and heard Seti's voice. "The Hebrews grew too numerous. They might have risen against us."

"Father, tell me you didn't do this," Moses pleaded.

"Oh, my son . . ." Seti said, holding him. "They were only slaves."

Moses backed away in horror. This man could not be his father.

The next morning, Moses accompanied
Rameses to the building site of the temple
that they had destroyed and that Rameses
was now in charge of rebuilding. "I will make this temple more grand, more splendid
than any other monument in Upper or Lower Egypt," Rameses was saying proudly.

But for Moses, everything had changed. Rameses' words were meaningless as he looked
around and saw the suffering of Hebrew slaves. On a platform above, a guard shouted at
an old man, "I'll make you move!"

"Ahhh!" cried the slave as the whip hit his shoulders.

Rameses was still speaking. But Moses heard only the slave's echoing cry and the
relentless cracking of the whip. When he could stand it no longer, Moses ran to the
scaffolding and leaped on the guard's back. The force of his weight sent the guard tumbling
far down to the stone floor below. He lay lifeless on the ground.

Then Moses ran. He had killed a man, an Egyptian. The palace was no home for him now.

But his brother Rameses followed. "Moses! Moses! Moses!" he called as he raced to catch up with his younger brother.

"Let me go!" Moses shouted. "You saw what happened! I just killed a man!"

"I will make it so it never happened," Rameses declared. "I am Egypt—the morning and the evening star."

But Moses turned away. "What you say does not matter. I'm not who you think I am!" Despite Rameses' pleas, Moses could not stay.

"Good-bye, brother," Moses said sadly as he took one last look. Then he fled.

Massive dunes of sand, taller than pyramids, and vast, empty plains dwarfed the tiny figure of a man, stumbling toward nothing. Here, there were no chariots to carry him, no companions or comforts. There was only the blazing sun, which looked down on Moses, a lonely figure in the vast, dry wilderness.

At night he huddled under a thin cloak, shivering in the cold. By day he made his way over rocky, desolate terrain. He stepped on a sharp rock, and his sandal broke. Then he tore off his sandals, his necklace, every trace of his old life. They meant nothing here.

But one thing he kept: a turquoise ring that Ramses had given him the night of the banquet.

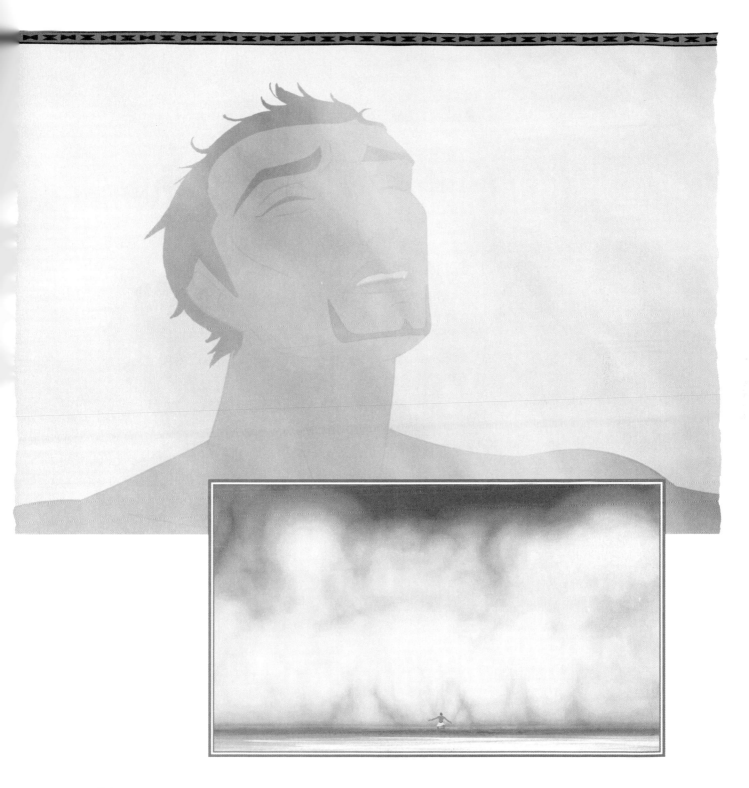

He stood staring at it as the winds began to whip at his shoulders and face. He barely noticed as a storm of sand pushed him down, swirling around him until the sand covered him completely.

Munch, munch, snort.
A determined camel snuffled
through the sand hills looking
for lunch. A patch of dry
grass caught its attention.
The camel chomped happily
and pulled and pulled.

Up from the sand came Moses. He opened his eyes just in time to see the camel spit
out a clump of his hair and trot away from its disappointing meal. He stumbled after
it and, with his last remaining strength, grabbed on to a saddlebag that glistened with
shiny drops of water.

The beast walked on, pulling Moses through the desert until at last they came to
a large trough filled with cool water. Moses plunged his face into the water and drank.
When he looked up, he was eye-to-eye with a sheep, who happily drank there, too.

Then Moses heard a child's cry.
"Help! Stop!" cried a little girl.

"Let our sheep drink!" shouted another.
Shepherds were pushing three girls away
from a well, wanting their own thirsty sheep to drink first. Moses stood up. Although the
girls were strangers, he wanted to help them.

Moses gave the beasts a whack and sent them running, with the shepherds in desperate
pursuit. Exhausted, Moses leaned against the well for support—and fell in!

The three girls pulled with all their strength to get the funny man out of the well.
Soon their older sister came to help them. But when she saw the man they had hoisted
up, she cried out in surprise, "You?!!!"

With a playful smile, the Midianite girl whom he had once dunked at the palace
banquet sent Moses tumbling back into the well. Her name was Tzipporah.

Later, hoisted from the well and brought bedraggled to the tents of the Midianites, Moses reluctantly allowed a group of elderly women to scrub him clean.

"Let me through! Let me through! I want to see him!" boomed the voice of a man.

As Moses wrapped himself in a towel, a large fellow with a warm smile entered the tent and hugged him. It was Jethro, Tzipporah's father and the high priest of Midian.

"Ah! You are most welcome!" he said as he lifted Moses off his feet. "You have been sent as a blessing, and tonight you shall be my honored guest." Then Jethro threw a warm blanket over Moses' shoulders and was gone.

    That night Jethro welcomed Moses with feasting and dancing. As the Midianites bowed their heads, Jethro said a prayer: "Let us give thanks for this bountiful food. And let us also give thanks for the presence of this brave young man whom we honor here tonight."

    "Please, sir," said Moses quietly, "I wish you wouldn't ... I have done nothing in my life worth honoring."

    "First you rescued Tzipporah from Egypt. Then you defend my younger daughters from brigands. You think that is nothing?" asked Jethro—and then offered his own reply. "You must look at your life through heaven's eyes," he said firmly, knowing that it was God who brought meaning to their lives.

    Once a prince of Egypt, Moses now found in Midian a new family, a new home. He learned the shepherd's life. In simple tasks, he began to see the pattern of work, laughter, and care that made up a worthy existence. And he and Tzipporah found love in each other, and they were married. The years that followed were happy.

Then one morning, Moses arose early. With a gentle kiss for the sleeping Tzipporah, he left to tend his flock—still feeling sleepy himself.

Seeing that one of the sheep had strayed, he went looking for it. He could hear its bell, but he could not see where it had wandered. Grumbling good-naturedly at the wayward sheep, Moses followed the sound into a small canyon. There he stopped, dismayed.

Before him, a small, bare thornbush burned with fire, yet it was not consumed.

Perplexed, he reached out cautiously, then put his hand into the flames of the burning bush. But his hand was not burned. Then a great voice called out to him. "Moses … Moses."

"Here I am," said Moses. He held out his staff
to defend himself, for he was frightened. Moses
looked around. "Who are you?" he asked.

And when the voice spoke again, the bush burned more brightly. "I am the God of
your ancestors. I have seen the oppression of my people in Egypt and have heard their cry.
I have come down to deliver them out of slavery and bring them to a land flowing with
milk and honey. And so unto Pharaoh I shall send you."

Awestruck, Moses dropped his staff and backed away, feeling unworthy and afraid.
"Who am I to lead these people?" he asked, offering excuses and doubts.

"Oh, Moses, I shall be with you when you go to Egypt," God said. "Take the staff in
your hand. With it you shall do my wonders. I shall be with you, Moses."

As these last words echoed, Moses looked up. The bush no longer glowed with fire
but instead flowered with new life. He paused in awe and silence.

Moses took up his staff and ran back to his Midianite home. He told Tzipporah all
that had happened. Moses held her face in his hands, searching for a way to explain why
he must return to Egypt.

"Look at your family," he said, pointing outside their tent to the Midianite people who
were working, talking, laughing—going about their daily lives. "They are free. They have
hopes and dreams—and the promise of a life with dignity. That is what I want for my people."

Tzipporah looked into her husband's eyes. She saw his determination and his goodness.
"I'm coming with you," she said.

And so they journeyed back across the desert until they saw the giant faces of the
statues peering over the soft sands. They were in Egypt, where they could see that the
Hebrews still suffered in slavery and unending labor. The sight of the taskmasters' whips
moved them and strengthened their resolve.

At last Moses and Tzipporah entered the palace. The air swelled with music celebrating the Festival of Ra, an Egyptian god. But the great hall grew silent as Moses approached the Pharaoh's throne—where he found that Rameses, not Seti, was Pharaoh.

Rameses ran to his brother with outstretched arms. "Moses," he cried, "I took you for dead!" For a moment Moses forgot his very purpose for returning. The love he saw in his brother's eyes seemed reason enough.

But when Rameses tried to welcome him as a prince of Egypt, Moses knew he must focus on the task God had given him. "Rameses, in my heart you are my brother," he said gently. "But things cannot be as they were. I am a Hebrew. I am here because the God of the Hebrews commands that you let the Hebrew people go."

"Commands?" Rameses replied, stunned and hurt by Moses' words.

Moses held high the staff in his hand. "Behold the power of God," Moses said, and he threw the staff down on the palace floor. Writhing and twisting, it changed into a snake. The crowd was impressed by the miracle, but Rameses was not.

"Very well, Moses," Rameses said dismissively. "Hotep! Huy! Give this snake charmer our answer!"

The torches were extinguished, and a low, ominous chanting began to echo through the hall. Then the great statues of the Egyptian gods gleamed in a pool of light as the priests chanted their names: "Mut...Nut...Khnum...Ptah...Hemsut...Sokar...Nekhbet...Ra!"

The show was dazzling. Lights, shadowy figures, and, finally, snakes that slithered up, down, and around Moses' snake, and even around Moses himself. Hotep and Huy were masters of spectacle.

Then came the most amazing sight of all. Moses' snake consumed the other snakes. Hotep and Huy proudly took their bows, not seeing whose was truly the greater power.

Later, Rameses and Moses spoke privately, without the crowds. "Do you still not understand what Seti was?" Moses asked his brother. "His hands bore the blood of thousands of children."

"Slaves," said Rameses.

"My people," said Moses. "And I can no longer hide in the desert while my people suffer. Rameses, you must listen. You must let the Hebrews go."

But Rameses said, "I do not know your God; neither will I let your people go!" Then he added, "Tell your people that as of today, their workload has been doubled!"

Outside the palace, the slaves grumbled bitterly at Moses. They threw mud in his face, and he fell to the ground. "Why don't you go back to the desert!" they spat at him.

"When did you start caring about slaves?" Aaron asked sarcastically. It was as if Aaron spoke for all Hebrews who doubted the promises of their so-called deliverer.

But then Miriam stepped forward. Her fierce gaze silenced the crowd and humbled Moses, who recognized her at once. "You shame yourself!" she said to Aaron.

Miriam spoke softly to Moses, but her words were as strong as stone. "God has never answered my prayers—until now. God saved you from the river. And saved you in all your wanderings. God will not abandon you, so don't you abandon us!"

With renewed determination, Moses stood and turned toward Rameses' barge, floating placidly on the nearby Nile.

Moses called out across the water, "Rameses, let my people go."

Rameses flicked his hand, motioning to the oarsmen to move the barge along. Moses pleaded with his brother, who finally cried, "Enough!" and ordered his guards to capture Moses.

But Moses moved first. He looked heavenward and, at God's command, placed his staff in the water. The blue water of the Nile turned to blood. People screamed, scattering from the river's edge.

"We are going to demonstrate the superior might of our gods," Hotep said, pulling red powder from inside his sleeve and throwing it into a bowl of water.

Even though the magicians' trick caused doubt among the people, Moses spoke without fear. "Believe," he said, "for now we will see God's wonders."

As Moses had warned, God sent great suffering upon the land of Egypt. God had commanded Pharaoh to let the Hebrews go, but Pharaoh's heart was hardened, and he would not listen.

So God sent plagues upon the land. God sent frogs, then swarms of lice and flies. Boils covered the skin of both people and beasts. The skies rained with fiery hail. The plagues were everywhere: in homes and streams and streets, in food and drink, in cattle and sheep. The plagues were even in people's dreams.

Before each plague, Moses again asked his brother to let the Hebrews go. Still Rameses refused. In the ninth plague, God sent darkness so heavy that monuments toppled under the weight of it as it spread.

    Again Moses approached Rameses. And for a moment, they remembered their lives as princes, switching the heads of the statues of the gods and getting into trouble—trouble they could always get out of. "Why can't things be the way they were before?" asked Rameses.

    Just then, Rameses' son entered the throne room, a torch clutched in his hand. "Father, I'm frightened," the boy said. Seeing Moses, he asked, "Why is he here? Isn't he the man who did all this?"

    "Rameses," warned Moses, "something else is coming. Something much worse than anything before. Please, think of your son!"

    "I do," answered Rameses. "My father had the right idea about how to deal with your people. And I think it's time I finished the job!" he continued, pointing to the wall that depicted the death of the firstborn. Moses knew that the final plague had been given form.

Moses returned to Goshen and told the Hebrew slaves, "The Lord has spoken to me again. The Lord said, 'Take a lamb, and with its blood, mark the lintel of every door. For tonight I shall pass through the land of Egypt and smite all the firstborn. But when I see the blood upon your door, I will pass over you and the plague shall not enter.'"

The Hebrews did as the Lord commanded.

As night fell, every Hebrew mother grasped her children in fear and awaited the coming plague.

Like a smoky mist of light that stretched down from the sky, the tenth and final plague swept through the city. Seeing the blood above the doors, the plague passed over the homes of the Hebrews.

But the plague entered the unmarked doors of the Egyptians and took the life of every firstborn child, with a sound like the gentle exhaling of breath.

No Egyptian family was spared—not even Pharaoh's. When the plague ended, there were wailing cries of grief throughout Egypt.

Moses entered the throne room for the last time. He found Rameses hunched over the lifeless body of his young son. As Moses watched, Rameses gently pulled a linen cover over his son's face.

Without lifting his head or turning, Rameses told Moses coldly and with immense pain, "You and your people have my permission to go."

Moses reached out his hand toward Rameses in a wordless gesture of love.

"Leave me!" Rameses shouted, enraged at Moses' touch.

Moses watched as Rameses bent down and touched his forehead to his son's.

As Moses turned to leave, Rameses raised his head, a chilling look of fury and hatred in his eyes.

Outside the palace, Moses was overcome. He stood silently for a moment, then bowed his head against a broken column, sank to his knees, and wept.

After his grief had quieted, Moses left the palace. As he approached Miriam's house, he saw her step forward from the doorway. Looking into her brother's eyes, Miriam saw the promise of freedom, but she also saw terrible loss.

Taking his hand, she sought to express all that was in her heart.

*Many nights we've prayed with no proof anyone could hear...*

*In our hearts a hopeful song we barely understood...*

*There can be miracles when you believe.*

The news spread quickly throughout Goshen. Pharaoh had relented at last and set the Hebrews free.

The Hebrews hastily
gathered their belongings and
loaded them onto carts led by
goats and oxen. With Moses in
the lead, the growing crowd
walked through the abandoned
work sites and ruins of the once mighty Egypt.

Softly at first, then with great joy and strength, the children began to sing,
"*Ashira l'Adonai*, I sing to the Lord!" Tzipporah and Miriam helped Moses lead the way.

As the Hebrews poured out of the gates of Egypt and into the desert, they sang and
danced. Among the thousands were parents and children, strangers and friends. In their
songs, the Hebrews gave thanks for their freedom from Pharaoh, whose stubbornness had
brought misery upon all of Egypt.

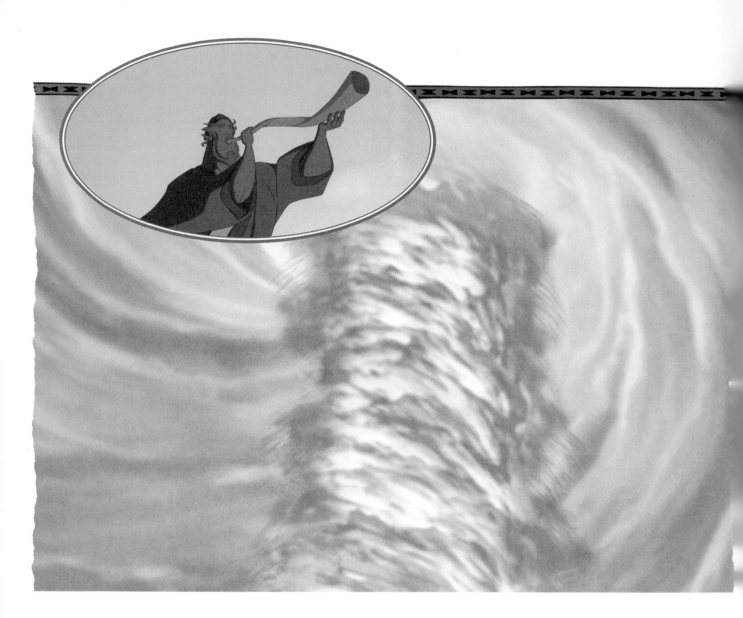

When the Hebrews came to the Red Sea, they rested a few days. Suddenly they heard a rumbling in the distance. A shofar sounded, and they turned to witness a horrible sight. Over a far-off hill, Pharaoh's army was advancing upon them. In panic, they turned to Moses.

Then, to their amazement, the sea itself heaved and boiled with a thunderous roar. In a furious explosion, a great pillar of fire burst from the water and flew over the heads of the Hebrews. The pillar blazed a path between the Hebrews and the Egyptians, blocking the army's way.

Again the Hebrews turned to Moses. "We're trapped here!" screamed the frightened people. "How can we escape?"

Moses walked toward the edge of the sea and looked at his staff, then up toward heaven. He again heard God say, "With this staff, you shall do my wonders."

Moses walked into the sea and placed his staff into the water. As the Hebrews drew back in amazement, the sea surged and parted, revealing a winding pathway between two towering walls of water.

The Hebrews stood awestruck and afraid. No one wanted to be the first to venture into that strange corridor of land in the midst of the sea. Precious time elapsed, until a tall, familiar figure stepped forward from the crowd.

Aaron walked toward Moses. His smile said that he no longer doubted and that they were brothers again. Aaron turned and stepped boldly into the cavern of water. The other Hebrews watched and then followed, making their way through the boulders and mud of the sea bottom.

Their path was treacherous. People fell and carts broke. But they helped each other. As the Hebrews walked or stumbled along, they looked up in amazement at the great fish gliding silently beside them, just a few feet away behind the wall of water. Moses urged them on.

On the far shore, the pillar of fire sank into the ground. For the first time, the Egyptians could see the parted waters of the Red Sea. Like their horses, the Egyptian soldiers were afraid—the miracle was too much for them.

Rameses shouted, "Don't just stand there, kill them! Kill them all!" The soldiers charged into the parted waters, with Rameses following in relentless pursuit.

"The soldiers! They're coming!" Moses shouted. As Moses and the last of the Hebrews climbed to safety, the walls of water crashed down. Every Egyptian was drowned, except for Rameses, who was flung back onto the distant shore.

"Moses!" Rameses shouted.

"Good-bye, brother," said Moses, looking back yet seeing nothing but the surface of the sea.

Free at last and finally out of
danger, the exultant Hebrews sang
of faith and thanks. They danced and
embraced one another. Moses approached his
sister Miriam, whose faith in him had never wavered. "Thank you," he said.

Tzipporah then stepped forward from the crowd. She put her hand on Moses' shoulder.
With joy and amazement, she turned him around to look at the great mass of Hebrews
in celebration. "Look!" she told him. "Look at your people, Moses. They are free."

As the Hebrews walked onward, they sang the "Song of the Sea." They sang of God's
power, holiness, and majesty. *"Deliver us,"* they sang. *"Deliver us to the promised land."* Their
joyful song echoed up to heaven. Many voices joined to praise God's glorious triumph.

The Hebrews wandered

for three months in the desert wilderness

until they came to Mount Sinai.

It was in this holy place that

God handed down the Ten Commandments,

the laws of right and wrong

for the peoples of the world.

*Moses was God's messenger once more.*

# THE PRINCE OF EGYPT

## HOW TO SHARE THIS BOOK WITH YOUR CHILD

Below we have provided some suggestions for families who would like to explore the story of Moses further, both as it is told in *The Prince of Egypt* and as it is found in the Book of Exodus. Shared family discussion can greatly enrich your child's experience of reading this book and seeing the film.

### QUESTIONS YOUR CHILDREN MAY ASK

Your children may ask you for help in understanding many events and themes in *The Prince of Egypt*. Before sharing *The Prince of Egypt* with your young children, you may want to familiarize or refamiliarize yourself with this important story. Anticipating difficult questions will help you provide more thoughtful answers, and your children in turn will get more from the reading.

Questions children will ask are likely to fall into three key areas: questions about God and God's actions; questions about death; and questions about faith. Teachers, librarians, local clergy, and other community leaders can be good sources of information and perspective in answering such questions for young children. You may want to engage your children in a dialogue about these issues by first asking them to offer their own answers.

## MORE IDEAS FOR DISCUSSION

Below are some open-ended questions that may help you begin and lead a family discussion. In addition, you may want to choose certain sections of the story to read aloud, inviting your children to pose questions of their own. The whole family can work together to identify meaningful themes and important ideas in the story of *The Prince of Egypt*.

1. What makes Moses a great hero? Can someone be a hero even if he or she doesn't always do the right thing?

2. Where has slavery existed in modern times? Why do people enslave one another? Why is freedom important?

3. Yocheved, Moses' Hebrew mother, puts him in a basket to save his life. Why does she do this? How does she express her love even as she sets him adrift on the Nile? Who else loves Moses in the story, and how does love affect his life?

4. Moses finds out he was not born to Egyptian royalty but rather to Hebrew slaves. He feels that his life has been a lie. Why would he feel this way? How could his adoptive parents have helped him feel more secure?

5. Moses learns throughout the story. From whom does he learn, and what does he learn? What important lesson have you learned recently in your own life?

6. Miriam maintains her faith and loyalty throughout the story. Why is her belief so strong? Do you know people like Miriam, who are faithful and loyal? What gives them their strength?

7. What miracles happen in the story? Why are the miracles important?

8. At the burning bush, when God calls Moses to return to Egypt, he resists. What reasons does he give for being "the wrong messenger"? How does God convince Moses to accept the task?

9. The story includes several children. What role does each child play in the story? How do the children change as they grow up?

10. What is the most important message of the story of the Exodus to you? Why?

## SOURCES FOR FURTHER INFORMATION

The filmmakers consulted with countless written sources, as well as historians, Egyptologists, anthropologists, scholars, and religious leaders. The following is a list of some of the written texts that were most illuminating and of general interest.

*The Bible* (New Revised or New International Version)
*The Five Books of Moses,* translated by Everett Fox
*The Qu'ran* (available in translation)
*Reading The Book: Making the Bible a Timeless Text,* by Burton L. Visotsky
*Egypt, Canaan, and Israel in Ancient Times,* by Donald B. Redford

For additional ideas, parents may want to consult their Bible, as well as other resources available from religious leaders, the Internet, and the local library.

## A NOTE ABOUT THIS BOOK

The story of Moses has been retold in many different versions throughout history and around the world. In creating this book, certain historical and artistic license was taken, as with the motion picture *The Prince of Egypt.* This book is intended to reflect the motion picture faithfully.

The biblical retelling of the story of Moses can be found in the Book of Exodus.